I Can Find It!™

DreamWorks

Shrek the Third™

Adaptation Written by Judy Katschke
Illustrations by Mada Design, Inc.

Meredith® Books
Des Moines, Iowa

It's good to be king—but not for Shrek. He hates wearing fancy clothes and eating fancy foods. When the royal banquet turns into a royal mess, Shrek just wants to go home to the swamp.
Find these things:
APPLES
DONKEY
FLOWER VASE
FLAMING SKEWER
FEATHER
HAM
SALT AND PEPPER
DRUMSTICK

Shrek, Donkey, and Puss set sail to find Artie, the heir to the throne. Fiona gives Shrek a goodbye kiss and big news—he's going to be a dad.
Find these things:
SHIP CAPTAIN
SAILBOAT
3 BLIND MICE
DRAGON
WHEEL
SMOKE LETTERS
LANTERN
bye

T.N.T

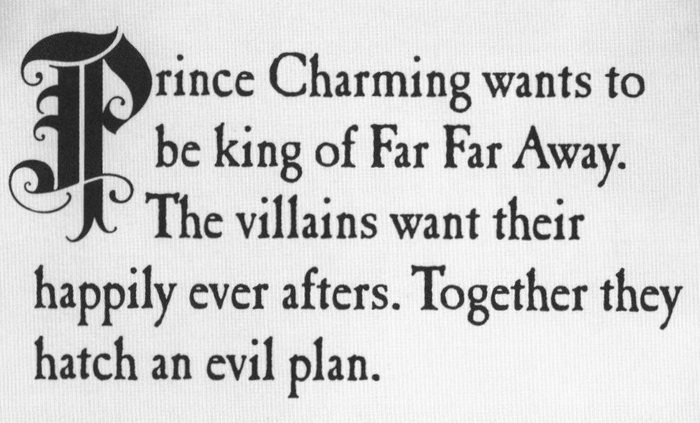

Prince Charming wants to be king of Far Far Away. The villains want their happily ever afters. Together they hatch an evil plan.

Find these things:

STOOL

MICE

SKULL CANDLES

SIGN

YELLOW-STRIPED BALL

LIL' RED

PIANO

BOTTLE

Geeks rule, knights duel at Worchestershire Academy. Artie decides to leave and head to Far Far away—with a little help from Shrek.

Find these things:

- DRUM
- SIGN
- POM-POMS
- PENNANT
- WOOD SWORD
- SANDWICH
- TUBA
- PAPER AIRPLANE

WEASELS
KEEP OFF GRASS
ser
sale

Prince Charming and his gang of villains invade Far Far Away. Next stop—the castle! And this time no one will stand in their way.

Find these things:

CUPCAKES

MAILBOX

BOY WITH ICE CREAM

SHOPPING BAG

RUNNING MAIDEN

SIGN

WITCH

FAR FAR AWAY
YE OLDE CHOKLIT SHOPPE
FUDGE
I ♥ TREES

At the castle, Fiona's fairy-tale friends celebrate her baby shower with lots of presents. The gift giving will soon be interrupted by Prince Charming.
Find these things:
BABY BOTTLE
DRONKEYS
CUPCAKES
DOVE
3 BLIND MICE
BABY RATTLE
GINGERBREAD MAN
SQUIRREL

FAR FAR AW

King Charming's first orders—bring back Shrek. But when Captain Hook attacks, Shrek and his fighting friends send the pirates back up the plank.

Find these things:

TREASURE CHEST

PIRATE

PIRATE

PIRATE

PIRATE

CANNON

CAMPFIRE

Fiona and the princesses break out of prison. They storm the castle to stop Prince Charming and to ruin his evil plan.
Find these things:
BIRDHOUSE
DEER
BANANA PEEL
BUNNY
THE OLDEN TIMES
NEWSPAPER
GLASS SLIPPER
POINTING KNIGHT
SHIELD

THE OLDEN TIMES

Shrek and crew to the rescue! Charming is forced to take his final bow. Everyone gets their happily ever afters as Artie is crowned the new king.
Find these things:
CROWN
PINOCCHIO
NOISEMAKER
WOOD HORSE
3 BLIND MICE
GINGERBREAD MAN
CUP
MUFFIN

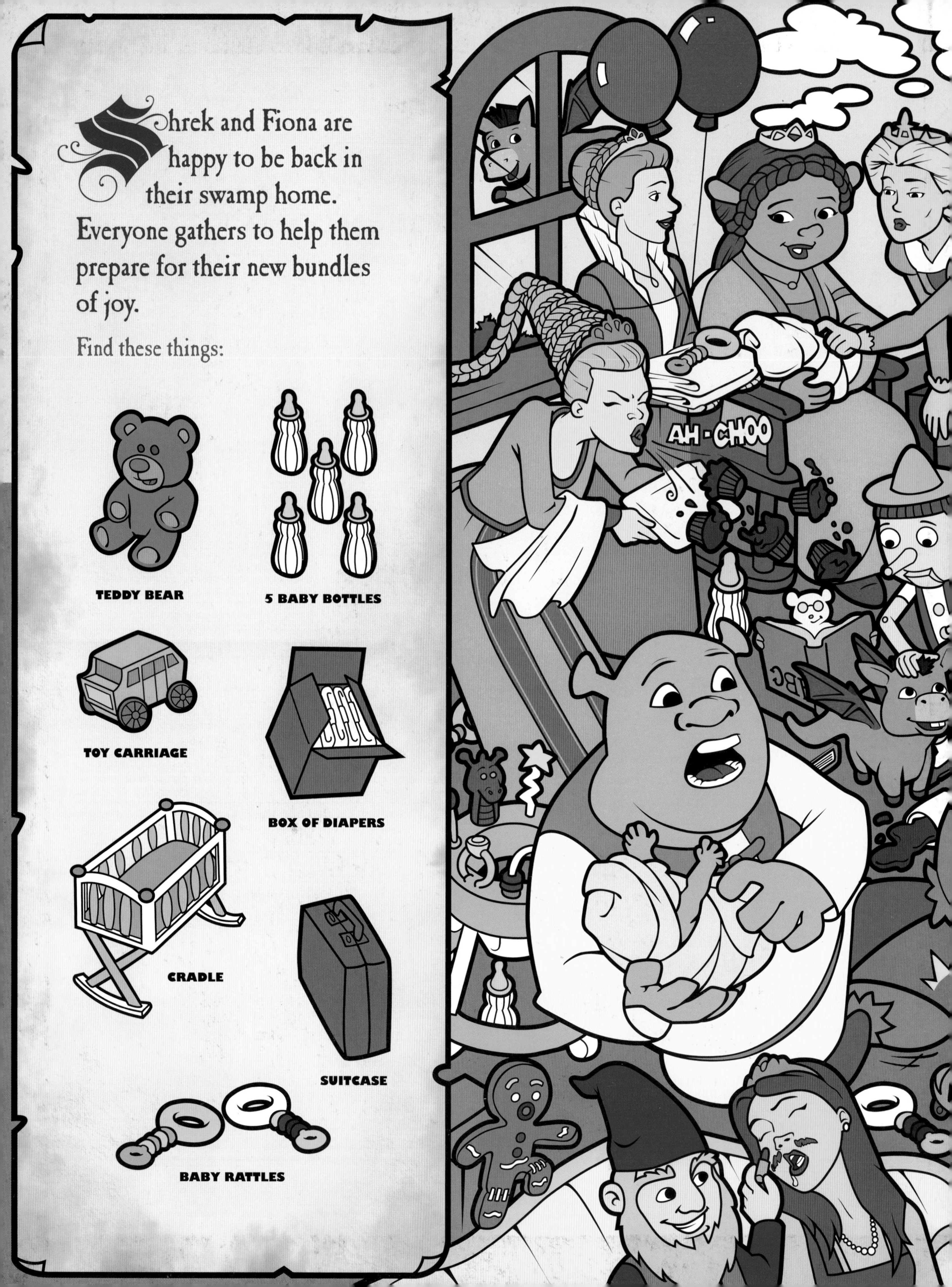
Shrek and Fiona are happy to be back in their swamp home. Everyone gathers to help them prepare for their new bundles of joy.
Find these things:
TEDDY BEAR
5 BABY BOTTLES
TOY CARRIAGE
BOX OF DIAPERS
CRADLE
SUITCASE
BABY RATTLES
AH-CHOO